For Tui. T Sutherland and Shannon Messenger for inspiring me to do this.
And for my great friend and editor E.R. (You know who you are)

PROLOGUE

SALIA STOOD SURROUNDED. FIGURES IN BLACK cloaks, hurting her. *Keeping her.* She couldn't concentrate on anything but the emotions swirling through her.

Fear

Sadness

Hope

Love

And Rage.

Just when her emotions bubbled up and she couldn't keep them inside her anymore, one of the figures lifted their hood. Just as her eyes adjusted to see the figure, the picture vanished. She jolted awake, threw back her covers, and waited.

Waited.

For so long.

Until she heard it.

What she'd been waiting for her entire life.

Salia jumped out of bed and ran down the darkened hallways, only lit by the fire pendant around her neck. The fire she longed to see. The hallways were silent, except dripping water off the ceiling, and her footsteps. She knew the risk she was taking. How much it would change her.

But it felt *right.*

It was all she wanted.

Down down down she went, following the stairs. Her legs were tired. She was exhausted. But she came this far to find them. And she would never stop until she did. Salia would always protect her friends. It was time to be the elf she always was, and is. Whispering filled her mind. They were close. *She* was close. She just had to run, not walk away. She was almost there. She ran and-

-Slammed into a big, gray wall.

She turned around, and the ceiling started crumbling around her. She would've never made it if her fear didn't boost her energy. She ran just as the rocky ceiling crumbled behind her. She kept running, her bleeding leg not stopping her.

Snowdrift? She transmitted.

No response.

Snowdrift? She tried again.

Snowdrift's mental voice filled her mind.

Salia? She said in Salia's mind

You're okay? Salia transmitted, relieved.

Yes! Where are you? Snowdrift transmitted. She sounded as relieved as her.

By the statue. The walls just collapsed behind me. Where are you? Salia transmitted.

With Sunshine and Leaf trapped in a room. We'll light fire through a crack.

Okay, Salia transmitted.

Seconds later, fire came through the cracks coming through a hallway. Salia ran down the hallway to find where it was coming from. She found the door, and heard whispers right behind it.

Are you here? Snowdrift asked.

"I'm here," Salia said, forgetting to transmit.

The door cracked open, and Salia tumbled into Leaf's wings Salia hugged them, and tears dripped down her face.

"I'm so glad you're okay," Sunshine said.

"You too," Salia said. Snowdrift was about to say something when something creaked behind them. Snowdrift and Salia turned around, and Sunshine and Leaf did the same. Salia's eyes adjusted, and found five black cloaked figures standing in front of them.

One holding weapons.

One catching Sunshine in a net.

One catching Leaf in a net.

One catching Queen Snowfall and Salia in a net.

One held out his hand, creating a ball of neon yellow flames, and threw it to a wall next to them, igniting fire everywhere.

ONE

S ALIA WALKED AROUND THE GLITTERING, MISTY

WATER pouring through sparkling rocks. The air was fresh. It was beautiful. Creatures of all kinds flew and walked everywhere. Salia knew where she was. And she belonged. In the elvin world. She was an elf, and she was happy about it. Glisteria was where Salia lived in the elvin world, with her parents, Kalista and Alvann. Glisteria was a sparkling, beautiful place. She always went to Glistaria Falls to have alone time. The main thing she'd been focusing on was finding who and what she longed to see. She had always read about what was beyond the elvin world, like dragons and the mysteries and the world. But meeting another big species like dragons or Alicorns would be amazing. And she always wanted to find them. Salia held up her home crystal, and leaped back to Glistaria, where Kalista was waiting outside.

"I was wondering when you'd come back," Kalista said.

"Why? I was just at Glistaria Falls. It's still in Glistaria," Salia said.

"Was… anyone with you?" Kalista asked. Salia couldn't read her expression.

"No. Why?" Salia asked.

"Oh. Nothing." Kalista said.

Salia was more than a little confused, and she was trying to figure it out when Kalista broke the silence.

"Well, I have to go. I'm going to go check on Alvann." Kalista said.

"Oh, ok. Bye!" Salia said.

Kalista leaped away without another word.

Salia had always thought it was confusing that Kalista insisted that she call her parents by her name. Salia had always considered... something. Adoption? Or something like... Salia couldn't bring her mind to the horrible thought. She tried to stuff the thought away and save it for later. Seconds later, Salia realized that she had to check in with Alvann, too. Alvann had recently been injured, by apparently trying to save a pterodactyl that flew away from the Sanctuary, and almost completely tumbled down a cliff trying to stop it. The Sanctuary was where they kept mythical animals to put them on a vegetable diet so they wouldn't eat each other, and to keep them safe. If a species went extinct, it would be a huge deal in the elvin world.

Alvann? She transmitted. Salia manifested her telepathy when she was 11. Alvann's mental voice filled her mind. He wasn't a telepath, but Salia could read his thoughts.

Hi, Salia!" Alvann thought.

Are you doing okay? Salia transmitted.

Yeah, I'm getting better each day! I'm just spending more time at the healing center at Jewel Academy! Alvann thought. Jewel academy was the elvin worlds' most prestigious academy. It was really old, and is still in the elvin world now.

Ok, good. Is Kalista there with you? Salia asked.

No... Why? Alvann thought.

Oh! That's weird! She said she was going to go check on you. Salia transmitted.

No response.

Alvann? Salia transmitted.

Sorry, Alvann thought.

It's ok. Why isn't Kalista there? Salia transmitted.

Not sure. Not a really good time right now... I'll talk to you later, Alvann thought.

Oh, ok. Salia transmitted.

Silence.

Salia walked into her bedroom at Glisteria, where her bedroom was bigger than one beautiful entire human house. The crystal chandeliers sparkled in the sunlight coming in through the huge windows on the side of her room. Salia walked in and layed down on her huge, fluffy bed, and closed her eyes. It was peaceful. But then, she heard something... odd. She jumped out of bed and peeked downstairs, where the sound seemed to be getting louder. Salia ran to investigate the strange sound. Louder and louder, closer and closer, until she stepped outside, where the sound faded. Salia was about to go back inside when a shadow appeared behind her. A black cloaked figure snuck around her house. Salia slowly walked around the dark house. Aaaaaaaand no one was there. But she knew *someone* had to be there. Salia ran into the shimmering bushes nearby and opened her mind to the thoughts around her. According to the rules of Telepathy, you couldn't read someone else's mind without their permission. But in special cases, sometimes you had to. Salia felt a faint sign of life. Too elf - like to be an animal. Something felt *wrong*. She blinked, and the thoughts seemed to be getting farther away. She began to walk back upstairs when the door opened and closed, leaving nothing behind but the sound of footsteps and the nature around them.

"Kalista?" Salia called.

No response.

Salia walked outside, looking around her. She was about to go back inside when she saw it; Kalista, pulling a huge purple satchel over her shoulder.

TWO

T HE SPARKLING PURES AND BEAUTY OF

Glistaria suddenly felt wrong. Whatever Kalista was carrying, it definitely felt *wrong*. Salia cornered Kalista and stopped her from going inside.

"What's that? Salia asked.

"It's none of your business. Now move," Kalista told her. Salia blocked her, getting frustrated.

"You do know I'm not going to stop asking, right?" Salia said.

"You want to know? Fine. It's medicine vials for your father for when he comes home." Kalista said.

"Why didn't you just say that?" Salia pressed.

"I'm tired. Now move, Salia," Kalista said. Her expression was colder than her ice blue eyes.

Salia sighed. Sometimes Kalista acted way more like a sister than a mother.

"You should get ready for Jewel Academy tomorrow," Kalista said. She was right. It was the day after the midterms, which was still a tradition at Jewel Academy. During the midterms, while the parents went to meet with the student's mentors, the students hung out and talked. There was always a huge party afterward. It was a Jewel Academy tradition. Salia's Jewel Academy uniform was a skirt with black leggings, shirt, vest, and cape. Salia was a level three at Jewel, just like her best friend Calalynn. Salia went to her bedroom, where her Imparter -- a small silver square that worked like a video phone -- gave an alert. Her best friend, Calalynn, had just hailed her. Salia hailed Calalynn and she answered.

"Hi! Are you okay?" Salia asked, immediately noticing the look of excitement and determination… and even… worried.

"Um, yeah. Salia, did your mom come home with a big purple satchel today?" Calalynn asked.

"Yeah, she did. I tried to ask her about it but she said it was medicine vials for Alvann for when he comes home." Salia said.

"Oh, how is Alvann, by the way?" Calalynn asked.

"He's good, but you're changing the subject." Salia said, starting to get desperate.

"Oh. Sorry. Anyways, I was sitting outside and I saw someone walking around in my yard. I thought it was my sister or brother being crazy again, but I realized it was your mom. So I was wondering if you knew anything." Calalynn said.

"That's… weird," Salia said.

"Yeah. I was just wondering."

"Yeah, I transmitted to Alvann earlier to check in with him, and right before I did, Kalista left and said she was going to check on Alvann. So when I transmitted to Alvann, I asked if Kalista was there, and he said no." Salia said.

"I'm sure we don't need to worry,"Calalynn said.

"Yeah, but it feels *wrong*." Salia said.

"Salia…" Calalynn started.

"What?" Salia asked.

"It's dinnertime. I'll tell you tomorrow at School.

"Tell me what?" Salia pressed.

"I have to go. I'll see you tomorrow." Calalynn said, and her picture disappeared before Salia could reply.

Now she was desperate.

Scared.

Happy.

Excited.

Determined.

And she would never give up. She didn't know what was going on, but she would do anything in her power to help her world.

Anything.

Nothing was going to stop her.

THREE

J EWEL ACADEMY WAS BUZZING WITH STUDENTS

glittering at school. Students hugging and greeting each other. When everyone started heading to their classes, Salia went to her ability session with her mentor, Lady Alouette. Lady Alouette was a tall, beautiful elf with long, blond hair. She wore a long white gown with an emerald sash. Her sky Leaf eyes shimmered in the sun.

"How was your midterm celebration, Miss Gailsong?" Lady Alouette asked Salia.

"Good," Salia said.

"Good. And I am very pleased to say that you did amazing on your midterms. Let's get started," Lady Alouette said. She had always been one of Salia's best mentors, and had always been so good to her. After her ability session -- which was practicing slipping past someone's mental blocking if they needed to -- Salia went to her locker. She opened it with a strand of hair, which was something every student needed to do. The lockers were opened by the students' hair strands so they knew that it was the student, and not anybody else. Calalynn's locker was on the other side of the level three wing, so she couldn't see her a lot. Salia went to Elvin History with Lady Renestrae, where they learned about the new Elvin - Ogre treaty. She then went to lunch, where students all over were buzzing in the sparkling cafeteria. Salia sat with Calalynn, who still had a look of excitement and determination on her face.

"What were you going to say yesterday?" Salia asked. Calalynn smiled.

"It's nice to see you too," Calalynn said.

"Sorry," Salia said, realizing how rude that was.

"Well…" Her voice trailed off when students walked by their table.

"Are you okay?" Salia asked.

"Yeah," Calalynn said.

"What were you going to say?" Salia asked.

"Salia, um, so last night something amazing happened. I'll just say… Last night I manifested as a Pyrokinetic.

FOUR

W AIT, REALLY?" SALIA ASKED.

"Yeah, I'm so happy about it, but…" Calalynn started.
"It's forbidden," Salia finished. "I'm so happy for you!" Salia said.
Manifesting an ability was a huge deal. "And I know what happened with past Pyrokinetics… but with your great power you can control it."
"I hope so," Calalynn said. "So this is me now. Pretending to be… a Talentless. Salia knew she was excited. She wasn't an Empath, but she could sense a hint of doubt, and one that stood out the most.
Guilt.
Elves' minds weren't stable enough to handle too much guilt, and it could result in a broken mind… or worse. Not that much was *that* worse than a broken mind.
"Oh, Salia? Do you think we're safe?" Calalynn asked. Salia was suddenly confused by the question.
"Of course. Why?" Salia asked.
"Oh. Nothing." Calalynn said. Calalynn frequently started a conversation, brings up something important, and then stops.
"Calalynn, I know something's going on. What is it?" Salia pressed.
"I--" Calalynn trailed off when it was time to go home. Calalynn walked over to the leaping crystal, which contained many leaping crystals,

adjusted the facet to Oceanus, waved goodbye to Salia, and glittered into the light before Salia could respond.

Oceanus always seemed to make Kalista really nervous whenever she went there. Before Salia was born, Kalista and Alvann used to live in Oceanus, and years ago, their underwater house crumbled, but was rebuilt, more beautiful and more glittering than ever. Kalista had never told Salia why it felt so weird to be there. Salia had asked many times, and her only answer was "The past is the past, but the past is still now." Salia thought it had just meant it was painful to think about what had happened, but Salia could tell there was something else. But what? She stuffed the thought away in The Things I Don't Want To Worry About Right Now compartment in her brain, to think about it later. Now, she had to worry about something else. Kalista had just hailed Salia, and told her that Alvann was open to visits. Salia found her mom's pathfinder to go to the healing center, and glittered away, letting the warmth of the light carry her to her father.

FIVE

ALVANN LAY IN HIS BED, LOOKING TIRED, BUT HAD A
smile on his face. The healing center at Jewel was amazing. Marble
floors that shone in the sunlight, and the beds matching the room
perfectly, with different color covers. Alvann waved at Salia.
"Hi!" Alvann said. But then Salia realized who he was really waving to.
Kalista wrapped her arms around Alvann and kissed him, and after a
minute, Alvann saw Salia.
"Hi, Salia," Alvann said.
"Hi," Salia said. Kalista gave her a weird look.
"Salia, your hair is a mess. Honestly, Salia," Kalista said. "Did you brush
your hair?"
Salia ran a finger through her long, blond waves.
"I was rushing." Salia said. Kalista sighed. Salia just wished they would
see her for who she was, not for who they wanted her to be. Alvann
cleared his throat, making them remember why they were there.
"I'm assuming you're not here to discuss hair," Alvann said. He held out
his arms and Salia ran into them. Alvann kissed her and Kalista jerked
Salia away.
"What are you doing?!" Salia said, turning to face Kalista.
"Salia, will you go home? Maybe get ready for School tomorrow? I'll be
there in a bit," Kalista said.
It seemed like Kalista's excuse for Salia to go away was to get ready for
School.
"Why?" Salia asked.
"I want to talk to your father. *Alone.*" Kalista said.
Salia glittered away without another word. Salia walked into the
shimmering home. Salia was about to go to her room when she caught a

glimpse of the purple satchel. She knew something was wrong. She didn't know what it was, but she saw a patch on the purple satchel Kalista brought home. It had a symbol on it. It looked like a bent star, with a big gold and white eye in the middle.

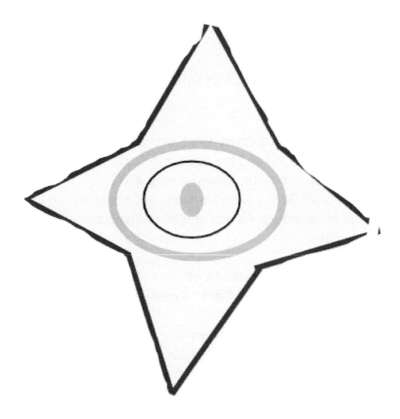

SIX

WHAT DO YOU THINK IT IS?"

That was the question she was asking. *What?*
"I… don't know." Calalynn said.
"I--" She trailed off.
"You think you know, don't you?" Calalynn asked.
"It… I--" So many questions. *So. many. Questions!*
"Okay, you need to sit down," Calalynn said.
Salia realized she was swaying.
"Come to my house after school? My mom will make Mallowmelt," Calalynn said.
"Yum! Mallowmelt is good. We need more Mallowmelt! The more Mallowmelt, the better!" Salia said. Mallowmelt was a creamy, gooey, delicious kind of cake.
"Um, Salia? Are you okay? You keep swaying and you're talking a lot about Mallowmelt."
"I am?" Salia asked. "Oh."
Calalynn laughed and wrapped her arms around Salia. "It's going to me okay."
"Thanks," Salia said, finally sitting down.
"Good morning, students!" Dame Loveene called, silencing the students for the morning announcements. Same things, like, telling the students to *stop putting curdleroots on my desk!* Along with other things. One thing caught everyone's attention
"You may not know this, but the following students and mentors will go to Everia tomorrow after school. Salia Gailsong, Lady Alouette, Calalynn Elrinia, you three will be going to Everia tomorrow. Thank you students, and have a great day!"
Dame Loveene stepped off the stage.

"Us?" Calalynn asked.

"I guess so," Salia said. What was going on?

Salia went to Telepathy, where Lady Alouette was waiting, in her long, purple gown with a silky purple sash.

"Confused, aren't you?" Lady Alouette asked.

"Yeah, why do they want us there?" Salia asked.

"I don't know," Lady Alouette admitted. "I guess we'll have to wait and see."

Salia was too nervous to respond.

"Are you okay, Salia? You seem… off, and it doesn't seem like it's from the whole Everia-thing." Lady Alouette asked.

"Yeah," Salia said.

"You can trust me, Salia. I might know more than you think." Lady Alouette said.

"A couple days ago Kalista came home with a big purple satchel and said it was medicine for when Alvann comes home. But last night I found a patch on the satchel that looked like a bent star and a gold and white eye in the middle." Salia said, letting it all out before she could stop it.

"That's… strange. Salia, did you talk to Calalynn about this?"

"Yeah. This morning. She didn't know anything."

"And she told me that you're coming over after school today. Correct?"

"Yes," Salia said. Why did Calalynn tell her? Did Lady Alouette ask her?

"Good. So when you go over, see if you can figure anything out. Then report back to me, okay?"

"Okay," Salia said. "Thank you."

After school, Salia went to her locker to get her stuff, and a note fell out of it. Salia picked up the note, and saw it was sealed with the same symbol on the satchel. She read the note, and it said:

The past is the past, but the past is still now.

Salia gasped.

Just then, she felt manipulated.

Exactly.

She was being manipulated.

She shouldn't pay attention.

Wait… wasn't that the same thing Kalista said to her multiple times?

It was. Salia started to wonder.

Did Kalista slip me this note? Maybe. But that's definitely *not her handwriting. So who?*

Salia realized that she should be at Oceanus now. She went to the leaping crystal, adjusted the facet to Oceanus, and let the colorful light sweep her away.

SEVEN

OCEANUS WAS AS BEAUTIFUL AS EVER.

The glittering yet intricate dome's 'stars' shone over Salia as she walked around houses that looked like coral. Seaweed with crystals and jewels sparkled. The delicate breeze through the dome felt amazing against her cheeks. Balefire cones of all colors lit up Oceanus. Salia walked across the floor, which was made of water with stepping stones. Salia stopped when she got to Calalynn's house. The outside looked like coral, covered with seaweed that looked like vines with sparkling crystals and jewels, although the jewels didn't really *look* like jewels. So looking closer, she realized that half the crystals were leaping crystals! The door banged open and Salia jumped, Calalynn was standing there giving her an odd look. Salia realized that she had a surprised look on her face. Or was it horror?

"What's wrong?" Calalynn asked.

"Oh, nothing." Salia said.

"Ok. Well, come inside!" She and Salia went inside together. The inside of Calalynn's house was even better. Every room had glass walls, showing the beautiful water around them. So many crystals and jewels and Balefire lighting the house. Colorful waterfalls inside and outside of the house glittered, which looked amazing with the glass borders. Calalynn led her to her room.

"So, I talked to Lady Alouette," Salia said. "I showed her the patch."

"Did she know anything?" Calalynn asked. Salia shook her head.

"I don't think so. Technically, she didn't say she didn't know anything," Salia said. "Just that I could trust her and see if we can figure anything out and report back to her. And about Everia tomorrow." Salia said.

"Oh, yeah, about that," Calalynn said. "Do you know why they want us there?" Calalynn's shoulders' slumped when she shook her head.

"Lady Alouette didn't say if she knew anything about that, either." Salia said. Calalynn didn't say anything.

"You're nervous, aren't you?" Salia asked. Calalynn looked up at her. "How could you not be? What if they Exile us?" Calalynn said the next part in barely a whisper, "Or me."

"Calalynn, what did we do that would make the Council want to Exile us?" Salia asked. "And why would they bring all of us if they were only supposed to Exile one?" Salia said.

"I don't know --" Calalynn started. After hours, they didn't figure out anything else. After School the next day, Lady Alouette met Salia and -- a trembling -- Calalynn at the leaping crystal center.

"Brace yourselves," Lady Alouette said as she adjusted the facet to Everia. "This is going to be very interesting."

EIGHT

E

VERIA LOOKED STUNNING.

The castles glowed in the evening. The delicate air of Everia felt so at home, and the glittering beauty of the castles and the entire capital. Salia tugged on her long, silky red and white tunic and nervously walked up the sparkling steps. Calalynn looked pale, and Lady Alouette's expression was hard to read. King Emete and Queen Lianna greeted them. They were each in different color attire, and looked stunning. Salia did a stumbly curtsy, and Calalynn did the same. Lady Alouette did a perfect curtsy.

"Miss Gailsong," King Emete bowed and took her hand. "Thank you for coming."

He did the rest to Calalynn and Lady Alouette, and took them inside the glittering palace. He motioned for them to sit in chairs across from them, and it mostly started with a lot of silence. Then, King Emete started.

"You are all probably wondering while you are here today," He said. "And I wanted to thank you all for coming. Anyways, I know you are wondering. So, I am just going to talk to each of you, and then you will see why you're here. Miss Elrinia -- his eyes lingered on Calalynn -- have you manifested an ability yet? He waited for Calalynn to shake her head. "Oh. Well, then. I hope something comes up soon, because it is still ability detecting."

"I hope I'll manifest soon," Calalynn said.

"Yes, and I'm proud of you. And knowing you, I'm sure you will not be… a Talentless. Be sure to let us know when you manifest, and tell us if it is an *interesting* ability, such as Inflicting, Mesmer, or Pyrokinesis."

Calalynn paled at the mention of Pyrokinesis.

 I will speak to you after." KingEmete said. Calalynn nodded, and tried to hide a single tear going down her face. Salia felt bad for her.

"Lady Alouette," He said. "You have been teaching Miss Gailsong here for quite a while. Correct?"

"Yes," She said. Salia did *not* like where this was going.

"Well, you have been doing a great job. You are one of the best teachers at Jewel Academy, and we know how hard it can get. So, we would like to offer you a position as an emissary."

Lady Alouette gulped.

"Thank you for this honor," She said. "May I have some time to think it over?"

"Of course, as much time as you need," He said. "Thank you."

Lady Alouette nodded.

"Miss Gailsong," He said. "Today we have something… very *important* to tell you. I understand that there is a new rebellion."

"Yes," She said. "The Starborne."

"Good. I'm glad you know. I'm just going to get to the point."

"What point?"

"I would ask you to figure it out together."

"Together?" She asked.

King Emete whispered something to Queen Lianna, and the beautiful blond Queen walked to a different room.

She blinked.

And there they were.

All this time.

She'd been waiting

Waiting.

Until they were attacked. With love. With hurt. With something she couldn't figure out.

But she didn't need to.

She didn't know why it felt different.

But it did. So all she could say was...

"Salia?"

NINE

Y ES, BUT THIS IS A PROJECTION," King Emete said.

"It is not real."

Salia watched herself in the clear projection, unconscious and bloody. Why would they show this?

But then she saw.

Five black - cloaked figures capturing her, and pulling her into the darkness. She glanced over at Calalynn, who was pale and had sweat beads streaming down her head.

"But… How… What…" She trailed off and cried.

Hurt.

Love.

Hope.

Evil.

That lost thought broke Salia's heart.

"This is a projection of you," King Emete said.

"Why would you do that?" Salia had to ask.

"We'll explain it all later." King Emete said.

King Emete avoided her death glare.

"This is what could happen if we don't stop them."

Salia laughed. "Wow. So, you're just going to send me off alone to fight a rebellion stronger than me?"

"Not alone," King Emete promised. "And you are stronger than them."

Salia laughed. "Okay… so if I die the first second I step foot in front of them, then…"

"We will stop them," King Emete said. "But we won't let that happen."

Screaming and yelling came from the shadows in the projection.

"Can you hear all of the screaming and yelling?" Salia asked.

"No. No elf has ever been able to hear a projection." King Emete said.

Okay, now this was confusing.

"But… I can hear it," Salia said. "You really can't hear it?"

Salia frowned when King Emete shook his head.

"None of you can, either?" Salia asked.

They all shook their heads.

"But… how? I'm an elf too." Salia said.

"Yes, and when we tried it with humans, they couldn't hear it either." Queen Lianna jumped in.

King Emete and Lady Alouette nodded.

"I… can't believe it." Salia said.

"We can't either. We'll look more into it."

Salia didn't respond.

She didn't want to wait.

She wanted to know what was going on.

"Just watch." King Emete said.

Salia watched the projection. It was kind of a blur, but it got her attention when they said the word "Ruthlessness."

"Ruthlessness?" Salia asked.

"Who said it?" King Emete asked.

"One of the figures," Salia said.

In the projection, Salia ran out of the shadows with the figures chasing behind her. Salia hid in a dark corner, and she immediately realized she was reading their minds. A figure ambushed her in the corner, grabbing her and dragging her away. Then the projection went dark

.

TEN

OW?"

It was all Salia could ask. But it was just a projection. She couldn't let it break her.

But... watching her losing to the rebellion destroying their world was enough to make her angry enough to want to stomp them to the ground. And especially that she was being interrogated without fighting.

"We need you to save us." King Emete mumbled.

"I will, but this is ridiculous. Just so we're clear, you want me to fight The Starborne alone, so they can kill me?"

"Of course not! Salia, you won't be alone. You will be with who you need to help you."

"And who are they?" Salia asked.

"You'll understand soon."

Salia didn't know how to respond. She probably stood there for an hour until King Emete dismissed them. She didn't say anything as they walked out of the crystal, sparkling palace. She didn't say anything when Lady Alouette asked her,

"Salia, are you okay?"

Salia could only manage a nod. Lady Alouette took her hand.

"You'll never be alone, Salia. *Never.*"

Salia felt a smile peeking in the corner of her mouth, but that wasn't what she was afraid of.

"What if I can't do it?" Salia realized she said it out loud.

"Then we'll all know how hard you tried, and everyone else you'll be with." Lady Alouette promised. "I also forgot to tell you. I know what that patch is. It's The Starborne symbol."

Salia gasped.

Lady Alouette nodded. "I'm hoping we can find out more about it. For now, I must go."

"You still haven't told me who I'll be with," Salia said.

"I wish I could tell you. But this information is highly classified, and even the King and Queen don't know. I'm the only one, and all I've told them is that you'll be with other creatures soon."

"*Creatures?!* As in not elves?" Salia asked. Did that mean she was going somewhere beyond the elvin world?

"I'll let you figure that out yourself." Lady Alouette winked as she leaped away.

Calalynn seemed to be avoiding her.

"Hey," Salia said. "Are you okay? You were acting weird in the palace."

"Oh, um, yeah, I'm fine." Calalynn muttered.

"You can trust me." Salia said.

"I *do* trust you."

"Then why won't you tell me?" Salia asked.

"I just haven't been in the palace in a while, and it was kind of… intimidating."

Salia nodded. "I get it."

Calalynn stared at her, opened her mouth to say something, then stopped. "How were you so calm when they showed that projection?"

Gah, she really wanted to stop thinking about it.

"I wasn't." Salia thought about the darkness or the projection. She knew it was fake. But for some reason, one word got to her.

Ruthlessness.

She shoved the thought far, far, *far* away into her mind.

"Do you want to come to my house?" Calalynn asked.

"Sure." Salia said. Calalynn nodded and pulled out her home crystal. Then she let the warm light whisk her away.

ELEVEN

HAT?" SALIA ASKED. THEY APPEARED IN A
place that she'd never seen before.

"No questions."

"Why? Calalynn, do you know about this?" Salia asked. All around her was lush green meadows, with sparkling waterfalls and trees. It was beautiful.

"I must've pulled out a different crystal. Sorry." Calalynn mumbled.

"But what is this place?" Salia asked.

"Just… somewhere my mom takes me."
Something about the way Calalynn hid her face in her hair told Salia that she was lying.

"Before you say anything, I'm not lying," Calalynn said, like she knew what she was going to say. "This is next to Oceanus. We don't have to leap."

"Okay." Salia said. Why wouldn't they leap? Something about that place made Salia shiver, even with the warm sun shining down on her. Calalynn mumbled something about organization and how stupid she was to pull the wrong crystal.

"Calalynn, It's not a big deal. It's just a crystal. If something were wrong with this place, you would've leaped us out of here immediately, right?" Salia asked, not trusting herself for saying that. Something had to be wrong. Why would it make Salia feel weird? Why was Calalynn so mad at herself for showing Salia this place?

"I guess." Calalynn mumbled.

"What's going on?" Salia asked.

"Nothing. We'll be there soon."

"Why won't you talk to me about it?" Salia asked. "I know something's going on!"

"Because didn't I just tell you..." Calalynn trailed off.

"What?" Salia asked.

"You don't belong here."

"I don't remember that!"

"You can hear a hologram, you have enhanced abilities, and you just don't seem to belong here."

"How could you say that?!" Salia was practically yelling now.

"I can tell you're mad."

"I'm not mad. I'm furious." Salia said.

"Fine. Salia, nothing's going on!"

Salia sighed. "Why don't you trust me anymore?"

"I do trust you! It's just that I don't want to start a fight!"

"I don't either. We don't have time. Let's go." Salia said.

"I'm sorry." Calalynn said.

"You don't need to apologize." Salia said.

Silence.

"I guess we should go." Calalynn said. "

Salia nodded and they started their long trek to Oceanus. They stopped when a crumpled up piece of paper fell out of the satchel Salia was carrying.

"What's that?" Calalynn asked.

"I don't know." Salia said. The note was inside of a crumpled envelope, and was sealed with a wax Gailsong residence crest.

Salia tried to pry it open, but it was too strong.

Salia gasped. "The envelope has Elves, Humans, Goblins, Ogres, Gnomes, Dwarves, and Trolls all around The Starborne symbol. It's from them."

"How do you know?" Calalynn asked. Salia finally opened the envelope. The ink was running, and it was all crumpled up, but she could still read it.

"This is a clue," Calalynn said, staring at the note. "It says 'The past is the past, but the past is still now.'"

TWELVE

HAT'S WHAT KALISTA ALWAYS SAYS," SALIA said.

"Whenever I try to ask her about something. And a couple days ago I found a note in my locker that said the same thing."

"Really?" Calalynn asked.

"Yeah," Salia said as her heart leaped. It obviously came to the conclusion that…

Kalista is a Starborne.

"Hey," Calalynn said, grabbing Sophie's shoulders. "It's going to be okay."

"I…," Salia's voice cracked. "Kalista had always been suspicious. Now it's time to figure it out. I'm fine -- she added as Calalynn started to say something -- and I will be. We have to do this. Together."

Calalynn wrapped her arms around Salia.

"Thank you," Salia whispered.

"Of course," Calalynn said.

Salia stood on her wobbly legs, focusing on not falling down.

"Also, I hope this isn't a bad time, but isn't it a little… strange that she insists that you call her Kalista? Sorry," Calalynn said.

"Yeah, it is. And you don't need to be sorry. She deserves it," Salia said, feeling her hands curl into fists.

Calalynn squeezed her tighter. "I'm always here for you."

Salia smiled.

"It's getting late," Calalynn said. "Let's go."

Salia nodded and kept walking through the dark night in silence, and Salia hadn't even realized it was night.

"Are your parents okay with me coming over?" Salia asked.

"Oh, yeah. Definitely."

The cold night breeze made Salia shiver. The grass rustled and the waterfalls left the only sound of the night except their feet on the grass and the wind rustling the trees and the grass.

"Are you going to stay at Glistaria?" Calalynn asked.

Salia swallowed the lump in her throat. "No. I really don't want to."

"You can stay with me at Oceanus. You can sleep over." Calalynn said.

"Salia hugged her. "Thank you."

"Of course."

Salia grabbed onto Calalynn's hand, Calalynn held out her home crystal, and they leaped away.

THIRTEEN

E

VERY PART OF OCEANUS GLITTERED WITH

every step they took.

"Where am I sleeping?"

"You can stay in the guest room. I don't think you want to see my bedroom. I totally scorched it."

Salia gulped.

"I'm so glad you're here!" Calalynn's mom came running outside to greet them.

"Thank you!" Salia said as she wrapped her in a hug.

Walking through the glittering home was amazing. The guest room was beautiful. Water everywhere. It was so calming. The water sparkled like stars.

"We'll get you situated," Calalynn said.

"Thank you, Calalynn." Salia said and smiled.

"You're welcome!" Calalynn accidentally sparked a flame, but closed her hand into a fist to put it out."You don't have to go back to Glistaria, you know. Unless there's stuff you need."

"Yeah, I don't plan to go back there unless I have to," Salia said. "But you're right, there is still stuff I need there."

"Well, you don't have to worry too much about clothes, because when it comes to shopping, my mom and I are stars. But you can still keep your clothes, of course."

Salia smiled. Then remembered the one thing she couldn't sleep without.

Snowdrift.

Snowdrift was the stuffed Dragon she couldn't sleep without. She knew it was silly, but she'd been so attached to her that she couldn't sleep without. And it seemed like all of her friends were sleeping with stuffed animals, too.

"Snowdrift," Salia whispered. "The stuffed dragon I can't sleep without."

"Oh, ok!" I can ask my parents --"

"It's okay. I can go. I don't want to put you in danger."

"Salia, it's fine. One of us has to go with you."

"Okay," Salia said. "Will you ask?"

Calalynn nodded and left the beautiful room.

About five minutes later, Calalynn poked her head back into Salia's room.

"I'm going to go with you. My mom is *exhausted* and my dad is busy.

"Okay," Salia said.

Salia walked downstairs with Calalynn. Salia took her hand, pulled out her home crystal, and they glittered into the light to go to Glistaria. The warmth of the light leap sometimes made Salia never want to leave. When they stepped into Glistaria, she felt a rush of empty, coldness against her. Glistaria was empty, which gave Salia the perfect chance to pack up her things. Salia went up to her old bedroom, where she grabbed all of her stuff and shoved it into a bag. She grabbed what she needed and loved while Calalynn kept lookout, squeezed Snowdrift tight, and ran down the stairs.

"Ready," Salia said.

"Okay, let's go. I'm tired."

"Sorry. I know it's really late."

"It's ok. At least today wasn't boring!"

Calalynn was still trembling.

Salia thought there were a *lot* of reasons to worry right now. Salia hugged Calalynn.

"Are you okay?" She asked."

"Yeah. I'm just *really* tired."

"I'm sorry." Salia said.

"It's okay. Let's go."

Salia and Calalynn leaped back to Oceanus, where Calalynn's mom was waiting outside for them. She looked worried.

"What's going on?" Salia asked.

"It... seems someone was here," She said.

Salia swallowed the lump in her throat. "Who?"

"I don't know… but someone in a black cloak ran through here. I vanished to get closer, and she had her hood up."

"*She?!*" Salia and Calalynn asked in unison.

"Yes. I caught a glimpse of her face and hair. She was carrying a big purple satchel.

FOURTEEN

DID THE SATCHEL HAVE THE PATCH OF THE

Starborne on it?" Calalynn asked.

She shook her head. "But there was a marking where it used to be."

Salia sucked in a breath she'd been holding. "Kalista."

"It's likely. Does she have ice blue eyes?"

Salia nodded.

"When she turned to face me, I got a glimpse of that, too. As soon as she saw me, she light leaped away. I tried to follow her, but she was gone too fast."

"Do you think she went back to Glistaria?" Salia asked.

"It's possible. But if I had to guess, I'd say she went to one of The Starborne hideouts." She said.

"Yes, and it is late. Go to sleep so we can see everyone tomorrow."

They all walked inside, and went to their bedrooms.

"What's it like being a Pyrokinetic under *water?*" Salia asked.

Calalynn paused. "Weird. Sleep tight."

Salia smiled. "I'm sure it is," She said. "You too."

Salia got into bed, but didn't go to sleep. Something shined in the pocket of her bag, and she crawled out of bed to look at it.

Her heart leaped when she realized what it was.

A note.

She picked it up and opened it, where writing was scribbled onto the piece of paper. It said,

It will rise by the end of night. Five creatures born to end the fight. Fight or Die. Help or Lie. It will rise at the end of night.

"What?" Salia whispered. This didn't have The Starborne symbol on it. Was it from the Starborne?

Someone knocked on the door. Salia jumped back into bed, pulled the covers over her, letting whoever was outside come in to think she was asleep. The door quietly opened. Calalynn's mom's soft voice whispered,

"Sleep tight."

Salia smiled, closed her eyes, clutched Snowdrift, but didn't fall asleep.

Snowdrift was from Salia's other favorite book series, Wings Of Fire. Salia knew the dragons, tribes, and everything else could be real. Salia started to fall asleep when someone called her name.

Salia.

Salia knew it wasn't coming from outside her door. She tracked the thoughts of any consciousness nearby.

Her mom, Her dad, Calalynn, and...

Something bigger.

Salia jumped out of bed and tiptoed out the door, and went outside of Oceanus, where the cold wind blew against her. The thoughts got louder.

Help.

Where are you? Salia transmitted.

Ice.

Ice? She asked.

Yes.

Who are you? Salia asked.

Dragon.

Salia's heart leaped.

Where are you? She asked.

Yes. Near shadows.

Salia sucked in a breath.

Are you okay? Salia asked.

Salia. I need you.

Why? Salia asked.

You can help.

Who are you? Salia asked again.

I gave you the note that said "It will rise at the end of night. Five creatures born to end the fight. Fight or Die. Help of Lie. It will rise at the end of night."

What does that mean? Salia asked.

It's our new Prophecy.

"Prophecy," Salia whispered.

What's your name? Salia asked.

See for yourself.

Something in the shadows flicked it's icy, spiky tail.

Salia slowly walked over, and the creature crawled out of the shadows.

Salia was face to face with a dragon. But not just any dragon.

Snowdrift.

FIFTEEN

I T'S... REALLY YOU?" SALIA ASKED.

"Yes."
"I --"
Salia hugged Snowdrift's icy, beautiful neck. Her icy wings glittered in the sunrise. Her wings were huge, and beautiful. Snowdrift wrapped her head and wings around Salia's back.
"We need you," Snowdrift told Salia. "You can help us."
"That was what the elves just told me."
Then it clicked.
"We?" Salia asked.
"Yes."
Two other glittering dragons crawled out of the shadows. One FlowerWing, and Salia immediately recognized her.
"Honey?"
"Yes. It's me."
The other was a SunWing, one of Salia's favorites.
"Sunshine?"
"Yes. Hi, Salia! I can't believe it's you!" Honey and Sunshine walked over to Salia and wrapped their wings around her back.
"I can't believe it's really all of you," Salia said.
"We can't believe it's you." Snowdrift said.
"Wait, are you the other creatures in the Prophecy?" Salia asked.
"Yes." Honey said and wrapped her wings around Salia.
"Who are the others?" Salia asked.

"You and Leaf."

"Leaf the CrystalWing?"

"Yes."

Before she could answer, Leaf launched into the sky. Under the sun, his scales were any color. He landed and wrapped his wings around her back.

"Leaf?"

"Yes! Hi!" Leaf did loop - de - loops in the cool air.

Snowdrift's icy scales glittered in the sunrise. Her beautiful crown sparkled like a castle made of ice. Which was probably right, considering her castle *was* made out of ice.

Honey's orange - gold and black scales looked beautiful. Her four wings had a beautiful pattern.

Sunshine's leaf - like wings made Salia feel so at home. Her green and brown scales were beautiful.

Leaf was as beautiful and gentle as a butterfly. His silky wings were any color under the sun, except black. His Leaf scales glittered in the sunrise.

"I'm the only elf in the Prophecy?" Salia asked.

"Does that bother you?"

"No, I love it. What fight does the Prophecy talk about?" Salia asked.

"Peace between species. Of all kinds."

"We can do this. Together." Salia said.

"Forever." Sunshine said.

Then it clicked.

"How can I understand you? Or how can you understand me?" Salia asked.

"We can understand you because you are speaking our language. You always have been."

"Does that mean… I'm a Polyglot?"

"Yes."

"Wow," Salia said. "We need to go to Glistaria."

"Why?"

"To find out what my mom, Kalista is planning. That will help start the fight for peace."

Honey lowered her wings. "Hop on."

Salia climbed onto Honey's back, and the five of them launched into the air. The cool air grazed against her. She loved it. They landed in Glistaria, and the light was on inside. She hopped off of Honey's back.

"We're here." Snowdrift said.

"Thank you." Salia said. She walked in, and an angry Kalista was there.

"Where have you been?" Kalista asked.

"I could ask you the same thing," Salia said. "You're a Starborne."

"I was wondering when you would figure that out."

"Well, I did. And I'm leaving." Salia said.

Kalista snorted. "And where would you possibly go?"

"That's none of your business." Salia said.

"Actually, it is my business." Kalista said.

"How about telling me a secret?" Salia said.

"And what makes you think I would do that?" Kalista asked.

"I think I deserve it." Salia said.

"Fine. *One.* But it can't be about The Starborne. Deal?"

"Deal." Salia said, letting it slip before she could stop it. There were so many questions about The Starborne. But there was one question she needed to know.

"Why can't I call you 'mom?'" Salia asked.

The silence that followed gave Salia chills.

"Because I'm not your mother."

SIXTEEN

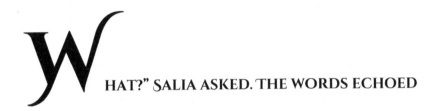

HAT?" SALIA ASKED. THE WORDS ECHOED

through her mind. "Who are you?"

"No more questions." Kalista said.

But she had so many questions. It all made sense.

Kalista had insisted that she call her Kalista.

She acted more like a sister.

Kalista always treated her badly.

"I'm leaving." Salia said.

"Good." Kalista said.

"I never wanted to be your daughter. Or a part of your family." Salia said. "You betrayed me. And everyone. I'm glad I'm not your daughter."

She knew that sounded cruel. But Kalista deserved it.

"Lucky for you, you're not," Kalista said. "And I'm sure we'll meet again."

"You might be right. But I will never stop fighting." Salia said as she walked out of Glistaria. She tried to fight back her sobs, but she wrapped her arms around Honey, and cried.

"It's okay," Snowdrift said.

"We're here." Leaf said.

Honey and Sunshine wrapped their wings around her.

"Thank you," Salia said.

"Forever." Sunshine said.

"We should bring her to our homes," Leaf said.

"I get to live with you now?" Salia asked.

"Of course. Firetail and Falltail are your homes."

"And the elvin world, but I think you'll figure out that you belong in Firetail and Falltail."

"Yes," Salia said. "I'm so excited!"

"We are too!" Leaf said as he launched into the sky.

Salia climbed back onto Honey's back and they launched into the sky. The dark sky was still dark, but the sun was rising.

"What does the first part of the Prophecy mean? When it says 'It will rise at night'?" Salia asked.

"It means that either a fight or peace could rise. And whenever fights or peace rises, it's at night." Sunshine said.

"That's what I thought. It's beautiful here," Salia said.

"Yes it is. We love it here. We think you'll love it too." Honey said.

"I know I'll love it," Salia said.

Then it clicked.

"If Kalista isn't my mom, then who is?" Salia asked.

"I think you'll find out soon." Snowdrift said.

Salia had theories, but one stuck out the most.

Now that she was a Polyglot, she could translate any language.

Alouette is French. It isn't her real name.

So was Lady Alouette... Salia's mother?

No. It's not possible. That's just a conclusion without any evidence.

But... Lady Alouette always felt like family.

"You think you know, don't you?" Leaf asked.

"Lady Alouette," Salia said.

"Oh, *her.* She's not your mother." Sunshine said.

Salia wasn't sure if she was relieved or sad.

But she knew that didn't seem right.

"Here we are." Honey said.

Firetail's dragon shaped island was beautiful. It was *huge.* But it was perfect. It was amazing. It was beautiful.

"It's beautiful!" Salia said.

"Yes, it is! It's amazing." Snowdrift said.

Salia watched the beautiful dragons fly through the air, into their home.

"Let's go to MoonWing." Snowdrift said.

"What's MoonWing?" Salia asked.

"It's where those in the Prophecy stay. Together, we are MoonWings."

"It's amazing." Salia said. They brought her to a beautiful, icy treehouse that had crystals and jewels around it, with beautiful scenery surrounding it. Salia and the dragons walked inside to the beautiful, huge treehouse with waterfalls and crystals. Salia sat on what looked like moss furniture.

"We know you're exhausted. It's Suntime, anyways." Honey said.

"Suntime?" Suntime was like naptime.

"Yep!"

Salia put her head down on the moss, and seconds later, she was asleep. She woke up feeling so much better.

"Come on! We're going to show you around." Snowdrift said.

"Okay!" Salia said. She climbed onto Honey's back, and they launched into the sunsetting sky.

"It's beautiful." Salia said.

"Let's go introduce you to some dragons!"

"Okay!" Salia said.

They landed behind a line of whispering, bowing and beautiful dragons.

"It's her!"

"I can't believe it!"

"The lost dragon!"

Salia thought they were talking about Honey, Sunshine, Leaf, or Snowdrift.

They brought her all around Firetail. The island was perfect. It was amazing. It was beautiful. They were flying back to MoonWing when Salia remembered something.

"King Emete said I didn't belong there. Do you know why?"

"Ugh, your royalty are never right." Sunshine said.

"Yeah." Honey said.

"I think you'll realize you belong much better here." Snowdrift said.

"Yeah." Leaf said.

"Yeah," Salia said. "I always felt like I didn't belong there."

"It's okay, Salia. You're where you belong."

"Yeah." Salia said.

"Are you okay?" Leaf asked.

"It's just… Kalista lied to me my entire life." Salia said.

"We'll never lie to you," He said. "We're here."

"Thank you." Salia said.

"Of course." Honey said.

Salia felt the cool air against her. Salia looked at the setting sun, turning the sky into a bright red, orange, yellow, pink, and black with sparkling stars. Salia knew they would fight together. Forever.

SEVENTEEN

S ALIA WOKE UP TO THE CHIRPING OF birds,

where Sunshine was waiting for her.

"What's going on?" Salia said as Sunshine flicked a bug off of her.

"We found something. Come on."

Salia followed Sunshine out of MoonWing. Sunshine brought her to a treehouse. They pushed the vines aside to find Honey, Leaf, and Snowdrift waiting for her.

"What did you find?" Salia asked.

"This." Snowdrift held a note in her claws and gave it to Salia.

"When we carried your stuff here, a note fell out of the pocket of your bag. We thought we would give it to you, but it fell out open and we didn't want to wake you."

The note said,

Salia, where are you? Join us now. If you don't, it will rise at the end of night. But it won't be peace.

- AG

"Alvann." Salia crumpled the note and gritted her teeth. "He's been lying to me too."

"Here, write back. Include a way of showing our prophecy."

Salia wrote,

It won't rise until there's peace. Where? Surrender. Stop lying. Never step foot in front of us again. We'll fight no matter what.

"There," Salia said.

"Perfect. We'll send Star the SunWing to drop it off." Snowdrift said.

Star walked in.

Her yellow - green scales glittered in the sunlight. She was beautiful.

"Oh my gosh, it's you! I've *always* wanted to see you! I have so many questions! Star grabbed onto Salia's hands. "Oh, right! I'll drop off this note. Want me to leave a *friendly* warning?"

"We're looking for peace, not war. But if someone comes after you, feel free to do so."

"Okay!" Star launched into the sky, and in a couple seconds, she was gone.

Salia had barely even noticed Leaf left until he came back.

"There's an elf outside of Firetail. Should we go check it out?"

"Yes. Salia, hop on Honey. Leaf and Sunshine, lead the way. I'll bring some guards." Snowdrift said.

Salia climbed onto Honey's back, while Snowdrift brought guards. They launched into the sky as Leaf and Sunshine led the way.

"There!" Leaf said.

"Get ready!" Honey told Salia. They dove down to where an elf stood on a small rock just outside of Firetail. Salia loved the wind against her as they dove down. Just as it looked like they were going to crash into the water, then swooped up and hovered around the rock, where the elf stood.

Salia immediately recognized the elf as Calalynn.

Salia ducked her head so Calalynn couldn't see her.

"What are you doing here?" Sunshine asked Calalynn.

Calalynn looked terrified.

"I came to deliver a note," Calalynn said. "I'm a Starborne."

Salia felt her hands curl into fists. Calalynn was now lying to her?

"How did you get here?"

"I saw a dragon and chased it away. It was breathing fire everywhere, and I tried to get past it. I'm a Pyrokinetic, so it didn't hurt me. I hit the dragon with fire and it fell into the ocean. I saw where it came from and followed it, and a security fire nearly killed me, but it didn't. Then the dragon dropped a note and brought it here because The Starborne said.

"Star!" Snowdrift said.

"At least we're already increasing our security." Leaf mumbled.

"Why would you tell us all of this?" Sunshine said.

Calalynn shrugged. Salia opened her mind to Snowdrift.

How can she understand you? Salia transmitted.

We're speaking her language. Snowdrift said. She snatched the note from Calalynn and gave it to Salia.

It's… blank. Salia transmitted to the four of them.

How? Snowdrift asked.

I don't know. Salia said.

"Guards, erase her memories." Snowdrift said. The guards flew around Calalynn, hit her with a sleeping dart, and erased her memories. Then they dragged her back to the elvin world.

Salia was furious with Calalynn.

"Can I see the note?" Honey asked.

"Yeah." Salia said.

Honey glanced at the note. "There are some specks that form a word…" Honey gasped.

"What?" Snowdrift asked.

"The ink ran, and when Star dropped it, it got destroyed. It's the same note that she was delivering, but they left their own note on it. It says,"

We will always fight, too.

EIGHTEEN

T HEY'RE NO MATCH FOR US," SNOWDRIFT said.

She set the note on fire and dropped it into the ocean. "We have to find Star."

Salia nodded and climbed onto Honey's back. "Let's go."
They launched into the night sky as Salia tried to see through the dark. They needed to find Star. They kept flying until sunrise, where they stopped on a cliff to rest. Snowdrift curled up.

"Are you okay?" She asked.

"Star is my best friend. I can't lose her." Snowdrift said. Wind blew against them, and Salia wrapped her arms around Snowdrift.

"We're going to find her." Salia and Sunshine said at the same time.

Snowdrift lifted her head. "Thank you."

"Forever." Salia said.

Snowdrift stood back up. "There's no time to waste. Let's go."

They kept flying, flying, flying, through the warm sun. After an entire day of no sign of Star, Snowdrift started to lose hope.

"We need to find her. I'm sorry, I know this is not like me. But she's my best friend."

"It's okay." Leaf said. How about we spread out? Queen Snowfall, look under water. Sunshine, look through the trees. Honey and Salia, look around from the sky of the elvin world. I'll look around from the sky. We'll all meet back here. Is that good?"

"Ok." Snowdrift said. "Let's go."

They all spread out. Salia and Honey flew to the elvin world, and stopped before they went in.

"Make sure no one can see you." Salia said.

"I will. It's night. I'll be searching the sky, and you'll be searching the land."

Salia nodded. They split up and began searching. It was dark, but some lights were on in some of the houses. Salia realized she should search Oceanus. When she arrived at Oceanus, it was dark. Salia had never seen it like that. But she recognized something. She saw Calalynn's shadow coming towards her window. Salia ran to the other side of the house, when someone called her name from the shadows.

"Salia, over here."

Salia saw Honey crouching down in some seaweed. "How'd you get here?"

"I saw nothing from the sky, and I needed to find you. So I looked everywhere and found you here."

"Let's get out of here before anyone notices us." Salia said.

She climbed back onto Honey's back and they flew out, they kept flying flying flying until they found the cliff. Everyone was there already.

"Did you find anything?" Salia asked.

"No." Everyone said.

Snowdrift curled up.

"We're MoonWings, remember? We will find Star. We have to."

"But what if she's..." Snowdrift trailed off, but Salia knew what she was going to say.

"We can't give up now." Honey said.

"You're right. I'll never give up on my friends."

Snowdrift spread her wings.

"There's no time to give up. I'm going to keep looking."

"Me too." Sunshine said.

"Same." Leaf said.

"Me too." Honey said.

"Me too." Salia said.

"Let's go."

Salia went alone this time, searching the cliff. Hours passed, and she didn't find anything but pebbles. But looking closer, she saw something dark.

A hole.

Salia poked her head through it, and heard what sounded like dripping water.

A... cavern?

She started pulling some of the rocks covering it off, leaving a space big enough for her to crawl through. She took a deep breath and went into the cavern. Salia kept walking, walking, walking, until something made her heart leap.

Breathing.

Salia walked around the dark corner to find a room litten by fire. She carefully walked around the ball of fire in the middle of the room and found The Starborne symbol.

One of their hideouts.

"Salia?"

She turned around and found Sunshine, Leaf, Snowdrift, and Honey standing behind her.

"What is this place?" Sunshine asked.

"I don't know. It's like a cavern! But I heard breathing, and found this." Salia pointed to The Starborne symbol on the dark wall. Everyone walked over to look at the symbol except Snowdrift.

"Breathing?" Snowdrift asked.

She turned around and found a statue of a dragon.

"That's... I don't know." Snowdrift said.

Before anyone could respond, rumbling came from above. Pebbles started dropping into the room, and they ran to see what was going on.

Rocks had covered the entrance.

They were trapped.

"Oh, no." Leaf said.

"Let's find a place to sleep. Just for the night until we can get out." Snowdrift said. She looked exhausted.

"Okay." Salia said. "Looks like there's moss beds here."

"Perfect. Sleep tight."

"You too." Salia said.

The dragons went to separate rooms just down the hall from Salia. Crystals hung from the ceiling. But they didn't make the room prettier.

It felt more like a warning.

Salia rested her head on the mossy bed, blinked, and started to fall asleep when more rumbling came from down the hall. Salia ran to see what was going on, but there was now a rocky wall separating her from the dragons.

Now they were separated from each other. Salia tried to fall asleep in the cold, wet, dark room. Salia fell asleep, and hoped that everything would be okay. Something moved. And again. Like a rock being pushed by someone. She thought it was The Starborne. She jumped out of bed and ran to the crumpled wall separating Salia and the dragons.

"The Starborne is coming. We need to be ready." She whisper - shouted to them from the other side of the wall. She realized she could've transmitted it when there was no response.

The Starborne is coming. We need to be ready. She transmitted to Snowdrift, Leaf, Sunshine, and Honey.

Okay. They said. She ran back to her moss - covered bed and put the covers over her head. She opened her thoughts to the creatures around her to track whoever was there. She needed to make sure it was really The Starborne. She felt life coming closer closer closer until it was just down the hall. She sat up in her bed, ready to fight. Salia would fight. For her friends. For her. For everyone. She wouldn't stop. *Ever.* Soon, she felt something sweet sting her nose, and saw a figure grabbing her. Salia's eyesight blurred and a raging headache occurred. Salia tried to thrash out of the figure's grip, but they were too strong. Salia looked up and caught a glimpse of the person under the hood. A woman with blond hair and ice blue eyes made Salia recognize her immediately.

Kalista.

Come on, Starborne. Salia thought with her last bit of energy. *We're ready.*

Then everything faded to black.

NINETEEN

SALIA STOOD SURROUNDED. FIGURES IN BLACK cloaks, hurting her. *Keeping her.* She couldn't concentrate on anything but the emotions swirling through her.

Fear

Sadness

Hope

Love

And Rage.

Just when her emotions bubbled up and she couldn't keep them inside her anymore, one of the figures lifted their hood. Just as her eyes adjusted to see the figure, the picture vanished. She jolted awake, threw back her mossy covers, and waited. They had drugged her. But worse than that, it was Kalista. But she couldn't let that stop her. She was ready.

Waited.

For so long.

Until she heard it.

What she'd been waiting for her entire life.

Salia jumped out of bed and ran down the darkened hallways, only litten by the fire pendant around her neck. The fire she longed to see. The hallways were silent, except dripping water off the ceiling, and her footsteps. She knew the risk she was taking. How much it would change her.

But it felt *right.*

It was all she wanted.

Down down down she went, following the stairs. Her legs were tired. She was exhausted. But she came this far to find them. And she would never stop until she did. Salia would always protect her friends. It was time to be the elf she always was, and is. Whispering filled her mind. They were close. *She* was close. She just had to run, not walk away. She was almost there. She ran and-

-Slammed into a big, gray wall.

She turned around, and the ceiling started crumbling around her. She would've never made it if her fear didn't boost her energy. She ran just as the rocky ceiling crumbled behind her. She kept running, her bleeding leg not stopping her.

Snowdrift? She transmitted.

No response.

Snowdrift? She tried again.

Snowdrift's mental voice filled her mind.

Salia? She said in Salia's mind

You're okay? Salia transmitted, relieved.

Yes! Where are you? Snowdrift transmitted. She sounded as relieved as her.

By the statue. The walls just collapsed behind me. Where are you? Salia transmitted.

With Sunshine and Leaf trapped in a room. We'll light fire through a crack.

Okay, Salia transmitted.

Seconds later, fire came through the cracks coming through a hallway. Salia ran down the hallway to find where it was coming from. She found the door, and heard whispers right behind it.

Are you here? Snowdrift asked.

"I'm here," Salia said, forgetting to transmit.

The door cracked open, and Salia tumbled into Leaf's wings. Salia hugged them, and tears dripped down her face.

"I'm so glad you're okay," Sunshine said.

"You too," Salia said. Snowdrift was about to say something when something creaked behind them. Snowdrift and Salia turned around, and Sunshine and Leaf did the same. Salia's eyes adjusted, and found five black cloaked figures standing in front of them.

One holding weapons.

One catching Sunshine in a net.

One catching Leaf in a net.

One catching Queen Snowfall and Salia in a net.

One held out his hand, creating a ball of neon yellow flames, and threw it to a wall next to them, igniting fire everywhere.

TWENTY

SUNSHINE RIPPED THROUGH THE NET AS

The Starborne ran away. She tore all of their nets away.

"Run!" She yelled. They tried to dodge the fire, which was causing more rocks to come down. Salia climbed onto Honey's back and they took off through the narrow halls. Salia tried to see what was going on around her, and tried to look for The Starborne. She eventually found a black cloaked figure running. They cornered her, and she pulled down her hood.

"Looks like you caught me," Kalista said with an expression that made Salia want to run. But she didn't.

"One step, and you'll be crumbled and burnt. And that's a promise." Salia told her.

Kalista laughed. "Honestly, Salia, do you think we're not prepared?"

Kalista's eyes flashed from purple to blue.

Purple to blue.

"Oh, stop it. My eyes are purple because of the Starlight Experience." Kalista muttered.

"What's that?" Salia asked.

"The process of becoming a Starborne. I only told you because you're going to be one of us."

"I'm never going to join you," Salia hissed.

"Keep telling yourself that. And we'll show you the truth."

"What truth?" Salia asked. Her pulse was racing, but she needed to know.

Kalista flashed a cruel smile. "How's this for prepared?"

Salia was about to say something when Kalista stepped aside, and revealed a girl with long, wavy blond hair with a black cloak on.

"Calalynn?" Salia said.

"Hi, Salia. Sorry, I --"

"Don't! You lied to me. You joined the enemy. You probably killed Star!" Salia interrupted. "How could you?"

"Who's Star?"

"I don't think you get to know." Salia growled.

"You left me without warning!"

"It's not safe there. For me."

"Why?"

"No more questions. And Kalista, we're sticking to our promise. Come on." Salia said.

Kalista laughed. "And where are we going?"

"To a prison. And Calalynn, come here." Salia said.

Calalynn hesitantly walked over to Salia.

"I --" Salia started.

Calalynn burst out laughing.

"What's so funny?" Salia asked.

Calalynn gave her the cruelest look ever.

"Come here, Calalynn." Salia said as Calalynn backed away.

"Why should I listen to you?"

"Because we have dragons. You can be dead in a second." Salia said. She couldn't believe she was saying this to her old best friend. But she deserved it. A loud yelp startled Salia and she turned around. Three black cloaked figures were attacking Snowdrift, Leaf, Sunshine, and Honey. Honey picked one up and dropped him in the air. She just missed him as she almost set him on fire. He fell to the ground and his hood fell off, revealing his face.

"Alvann?" Salia said. He was struggling to get up as the back of his hood burned off. He clutched his head in pain, and that's when Salia realized,

He was faking his injuries.

Snowdrift attacked two other figures that Salia didn't recognize. And then she understood why.

They were traitorous ogres.

"We didn't want this! We wanted peace! But you want to fight, you got a fight!" Snowdrift said.

Sunshine and Honey combined their fire to make a huge fireball running into all of them. It hit all of the figures, and kept going until it was a foot away from Calalynn.

"Stop!" She yelled.

Calalynn hurled her own fire at the ball, causing it to rumble and start shaking.

"Run!" Salia yelled. Everyone rushed out of the room while the dragons combined their fire to create an opening. Rocks burst apart and melted, not stopping them from squeezing through the opening. They burst into the air, leaving behind The Starborne. Seconds later, an explosion erupted the entire cavern, leaving it nothing but bits of rock and fire, and blood. They flew and flew and flew until they were just above the ocean. The beautiful, shimmering water didn't calm Salia down.

"Did we just... kill them?" Leaf asked.

"I would think so." Salia mumbled. "They deserve it."

"Are you okay?" Honey asked her.

"Yeah. I'm just so mad at them." Salia said.

"We need Star." Snowdrift said. "Do you think she's gone?"

"We can't say anything yet." Salia said. "I hope it's going to be okay."

"She's also our best fighter." Snowdrift said.

"We're here." Honey said. "I miss her too."

"I know." Snowdrift said. "Let's go back to Firetail. Everyone's waiting for us."

Firetail erupted with happiness, worry, and questions when they got back.

"Are you okay?"

"Did you capture them?"

"I'm hungry."

"My sloth has a name!"

"He stole my sloth!"

Salia couldn't help but smile at the little dragonets. Snowdrift did too. They walked into MoonWing, where a dragon was waiting for them.

"Mango. What are you doing here?" Snowdrift asked.

Mango's orange - pink scales sparkled in the sun.

"Your majesty," Mango said, bowing. "And Salia, the MoonWing. How nice to finally meet you!"

"Nice to meet you too!" Salia said.

"I have news for you. All of you." Mango said.

"Okay." Snowdrift said.

"Star was spotted last night. Some of our guards went to look for her, and saw her walking on land. They swooped down to save her, but she disappeared."

"How? How did she disappear?" Snowdrift asked.

"She was very hurt. She was limping. She must've taken shelter in a cavern."

"Why didn't you fly down to her?"

"We tried, but she disappeared."

"Did you keep looking for her?"

"We looked all night, and found nothing. Just remains of an old cavern."

Salia's heart leaped. The cavern they were at? Snowdrift must've been thinking the same thing.

"Where was the cavern?" She asked.

"On a cliff by the ocean." Mango said.

Salia couldn't breathe. She couldn't think. Except for one horrible thought.

Was Star there when the cavern collapsed?

Or worse.

Was she trapped inside?

"Salia, are you okay?" Mango asked. He was already trying to calm down Snowdrift.

Salia nodded, not trusting her voice.

"While we were searching, we found puddles of blood. Don't worry, not Star's." He added when Snowdrift buried her face in her claws. "Three elves, two traitorous ogres."

"The Starborne." Salia said.

"What?" Mango asked.

"It's a long story." Salia and Snowdrift said at the same time.

"You can tell me another time. Now we have some searching to do."

"For Star?" Salia asked.

"Of course."

"Let's go." Sunshine said.

"Your majesty, are you sure you're up to this?" Mango asked.

"Why wouldn't I be? Star is my best friend." Snowdrift said. Salia was amazed at how brave she sounded.

"Good luck. We'll be searching on the other side of the cliff." Mango said.

"You too." Snowdrift said.

"Oh, and your majesty? I need to talk to you." Mango said. Snowdrift followed him over to the trees.

"What are they talking about?" Leaf asked.

"I don't know." Salia, Sunshine, and Honey said at the same time. First Mango and Snowdrift started out as whispers. Then it started turning into shouts.

"How could you be so selfish? Star might be gone!"

"I'm just trying to protect you!"

"I'm trying to protect Firetail, The MoonWings, you, and Star! Please, Mango. I can't lose her."

"I know. She's our best fighter. But how are we going to save her *if* we find her?"

"You say that like you don't want to find her." Snowdrift said.

"Of course I do. I'll I'm saying is sometimes we need to take risks. And other times we have to save ourselves."

"Unbelievable. You know, I thought you would always protect her. Then, *you* volunteered to keep her safe when she went to drop off that note. Now she's missing, and there wasn't any security on her. Now this? Mango, we have to find her."

"What if it's too late?"

Snowdrift backed up. "Don't!"

"We'll talk about this later. Salia, come here."

Salia froze.

"What do you want?" Snowdrift asked.

"I want Salia to come here so I can talk to her."

Snowdrift growled. "Fine. But we're looking for Star."

Salia walked over.

"Salia, before I start," Mango said. He leaned closer and whispered into her ear. "You belong here."

Salia nodded.

"Was Kalista Gailsong in the cavern you were in?"

"How do you know about that?" Salia asked.

"I told him." Snowdrift said.

"Okay. But yes, she was."

"Okay. Well, then. None of them ever made it out of the cavern."

"I know. And?" Salia said.

"I thought you'd be sadder."

"Nope. She lied to me. *All* of them lied to me."

"Oh. Well, then. I must go. Good luck." He flew away without another word.

Snowdrift waited until he was out of sight. "How much of that did you hear?"

"A lot." Sunshine said. "Why? What did he say?"

"We shouldn't save Star."

"WHAT?!" They all asked in unison. "How could he?"

"That's what I said. But he acted like he didn't want to save her."

"We'll find her." Salia said.

Snowdrift wrapped her wings around her. "Thank you."

"Of course." Salia said.

"Let's go." She said. "Before it's too late."

TWENTY ONE

THE SEARCH FOR STAR WAS OFFICIAL.

They searched until they couldn't anymore. Days had gone by. But there was still nothing. Snowdrift obsessed over every moving thing. Salia couldn't blame her.

"We're not going to find her." Snowdrift said, burying her face in her claws. It was pouring down rain, and the ground had become mud, washing away their good chance of finding her. "The rain washed away all of the blood and the scents."

"That doesn't mean she's not still alive." Sunshine said. "Don't let Mango get to you."

Snowdrift cringed at the name.

"Why didn't he want to save her?" Salia had to ask.

"I don't know. He said it was about taking risks, but that doesn't make any sense. He used to always take risks to protect us and Star."

"Yeah, and then he clawed me and threw me off of a cliff!" Sunshine said.

"When you were little dragonets. But you're right. That took months of healing." Snowdrift said. Sunshine growled.

"What?" Honey asked.

"Someone's here."

Salia turned around to find the last dragon she wanted to see.

"Mango." Snowdrift growled. "I thought you hated the idea of finding Star and saving her life."

"I never said that." He said.

"Technically, you did." Sunshine said.

Mango ignored her. "I came here to see if you found her. But I guess not."

"We're trying to find her, unlike you." Salia snapped.

Mango laughed. "I'm doing as much as you are. I'm protecting Firetail while you're out on a little giggle fest with your MoonWings."

"Firetail knows where I am. And it's not a giggle fest! We're looking for Star!" Snowdrift snapped.

"Maybe. Or maybe your precious MoonWings are going to die because of The Starborne."

"They're no match for us. And how did you know about The Starborne?"

"While you were gone, I did some research. It's quite interesting. If only you were there to protect us."

"Mango, what is going on?" Snowdrift demanded.

"You tell me." Mango growled and jumped on Snowdrift, breathing his fire.

"Stop!" Salia yelled. Leaf and Sunshine fought Mango while Salia climbed onto Honey's back. They launched into the air and hovered right over where Mango clutched his head from Snowdrift, Leaf, and Sunshine's last strike. Honey got her fire ready, and the four of them combined their fire and hit Mango with it, knocking him back. But they didn't have long to celebrate their victory.

"Your skills are impressive." Mango said, breathing heavily. "But not good enough."

Behind him, creatures of every kind came pouring out of the woods and held daggers.

It took Salia a second to realize that...

"You're a Starborne?"

Mango laughed. "The first dragon. Isn't that great?"

"What it is is traitorous." Snowdrift said. "I never should've trusted you."

"And yet, you did. Finding your precious Star might be more difficult than you think."

"Where are you keeping her?" Snowdrift said. Creatures behind her put metal bonds on her. They did the same with the rest of them. "Where are you taking us?"

"Where Star is now. Dead."

Salia saw it.

The fear and rage in Snowdrifts' eyes.

The evil in Mango.

She wouldn't let that stop her.

Her anger bubbled up inside until it was too much. She felt like her head was going to explode.

"Let. Us. Go!" Salia yelled. In a second, everything around her went dark. She heard faint screaming around her and felt herself in the air. She was dizzy. She couldn't breathe. Then she fainted, tuning out everything around her.

TWENTY TWO

SALIA, WAKE UP."

The three words that changed everything. The hurt in her faded with the words. She didn't know who said it. She felt a wave of warmth wash through her mind. It was enough to make her open her eyes. Her vision was blurred, but she saw four concerned dragons around her.

"Salia! Are you okay?" Snowdrift said as she wrapped her wings around Salia.

Salia breathed in the fresh air around her and turned her head to look at the beautiful scenery around her. She was either in MoonWing or a healing place.

"Yeah, I'm okay." Salia said.

"That was crazy! You launched into the air and unleashed ten beams of light and knocked everyone in The Starborne back, like, all the way over the ocean!" Leaf said.

"Really?" Salia asked.

"Yeah! I remember Mango catching on fire as soon as the ray hit him!" Sunshine said.

"Then you fainted and we rushed you back here immediately!" Honey said.

"What about Star?" Salia asked.

"We needed to save you. We're going back to look for her later." Snowdrift said.

Salia smiled.

"Are you okay?" Salia asked them.

"Yeah. You only hit The Starborne." Leaf said.

"You were so pale, we thought you were dying!" Sunshine said.

Honey wrapped her wings around Salia. "I'm so glad you're okay."

Salia smiled. "You too."

"If Mango--" Snowdrift started.

"Did you capture them?" Salia interrupted.

"No. You shot them back too far." Sunshine said.

Salia felt sick. "How did I do that?"

"We should ask you the same question." Leaf said.

Salia gulped. "I don't know."

Was she inflicting? What happened?

"We need to find Star." Salia said, shoving the thought aside for now. She stood up and immediately sat back down with the head rush.

"But we need you. We know where she hopefully is. Can't you track her thoughts?" Sunshine said.

Salia forgot about that.

"I'm fine. We need to go." Salia said, standing up slower.

"Salia, are you sure?" Snowdrift asked. "You might still need rest."

"I'm sure I've had a lot. How long have I been out?" Salia asked.

"A little over two days." Sunshine said.

"TWO DAYS?" Salia asked. She frowned when everyone nodded. "Let's go."

Snowdrift opened her mouth to say something, but didn't.

"Very well. Let's go."

Days went by with no progress. Salia was sure Star was gone. But she had a feeling there was still something left of her.

"I'm going to track her thoughts." Salia said.

Salia tuned out everything around her. She opened her mind to everything around her. She felt the dragons around her, and was about to sever her connection. But she felt two other creatures. One with a strong life, but her thoughts were blocked. And one with the faintest glimmer of life left. Could one of them be Star? Salia could barely finish the thought when the stronger thoughts got closer.

Closer.

Until whoever it was was right behind them.

Salia opened her eyes and turned around, to find a beautiful woman in a long white tunic. Her sky blue eyes sparkled in the sunlight.

Lady Alouette smiled as she said, "Surprise!"

TWENTY THREE

HAT ARE YOU DOING HERE?" SALIA ASKED.

Lady Alouette was standing there with a satchel around her shoulder.

"I come visit the dragons a lot. I'm trying to make peace between our species, too."

"I-- It's just-- I can't--" Salia ran into Lady Alouette's arms before she could finish her sentence. "I missed you so much."

"I've missed you too. Good to see you, MoonWings." She bowed to Snowdrift. "How is everything going?"

"Mango is a Starborne," Salia told her. "He was with them a couple days ago. And Star is missing."

"Star?" Lady Alouette paled. "Oh, no. We need to find her."

"We've been looking for Star for weeks," Snowdrift said. "And still nothing."

"I'm sorry," Lady Alouette said. "I'm sure you were tracking her thoughts? I apologize for interrupting. Perhaps you could use a mental boost, Salia."

"She does, considering what happened a couple nights ago." Sunshine mumbled.

"What happened?" Lady Alouette asked.

"When Mango and The Starborne were attacking, Salia got really mad and launched into the sky. Rays of light shot out of her head and hit The Starborne back all the way over the ocean. Then she fainted, and has been out for a little over two days!" Leaf said.

All of the color drained from Lady Alouette's face. "Salia--" She started.

"I'm fine." She told her.

"Salia…"

"Let's find Star. Will you help me track her thoughts?" Salia asked.

"Salia! You don't understand! It's not safe here!"

"What?" Salia asked. "How?"

"What happened a couple nights ago happened to me when I first allied with the dragons! It's really dangerous, Salia."

"Why?" Salia asked.

Lady Alouette sighed. "Please, Salia. We need you."

"Does that mean I'm…" Salia couldn't finish the sentence. But they all knew what she was going to say.

Dying?

Lady Alouette shook her head. "Hopefully not. We just need to get you out of here. Not forever, but for at least a while."

"I don't understand! What's going on?" Salia had to ask.

"I'll tell you another time. Now we need to get you back to the elvin world."

Salia didn't have a *huge* problem with that, but this was all so… confusing.

"Please! I need to know!" Salia begged.

"Can I tell you something else?" Lady Alouette asked.

"Why? I would like to know your name."

"And that's *another* long story. I chose that name. And someday you will get to know my real one."

Salia was about to ask why couldn't she tell her now, but it didn't seem like it was worth arguing.

"Just tell me!" Salia begged. "I need to know."

Salia realized she didn't ask her about if she really *was* her mother. When the MoonWings told her, there was a *lot* of hesitation.

"My name or why you can't stay?"

"Technically both. But the second one." Salia said.

Lady Alouette took a long, deep breath until she finally said, "It could weaken your abilities. And worst of all, it's lethal."

TWENTY FOUR

HOW?" SALIA WAS CONFUSED. ACTUALLY, THIS was more than confusing. This was… *weird.*

"If you don't believe me…"

"No, I do. It's just… How? *Why?* Those are the questions!"

"And here is your answer. I will tell you all of this later in the elvin world. But now, we need to go."

"Please. Just let me look for Star. One more time." Salia whispered.

Lady Alouette gave her the saddest smile ever. "Fine. I'm going to help."

Salia smiled. "Will you give me a mental boost?"

Lady Alouette nodded and a wave of energy washed through Salia's head.

"Whoa. Thank you. I'm picking up so many thoughts. But one of them is…" Salia felt a lump rising in her throat. "I think Star is here."

"What?" Snowdrift asked. "Really?"

"I don't know. But I still feel the faintest glimmer of life. And it feels like dragon thoughts." Salia said.

"There's no time to waste. Come on! Salia, will you tell us where?"

Salia nodded. But when she figured out where, bile coated her tongue. "Are you sure you're up to going to where I think she is?"

"Yes. Anywhere."

Salia wished she didn't have to say it, but did anyway.

"She's in the cavern." Salia choked on the words.

"But… it collapsed."

"Not all of it. I remember some of it standing." Sunshine said.

Snowdrift sighed. "Come on. I guess we're going to the cavern."

They arrived at the crumbled cavern, which was now just rocks and ash. Salia opened her mind to Star's thoughts again. The glimmer of life was still there.

"Will you help me push back the boulder?" Salia asked them once they got to a spot that was still standing. Soon, they moved the boulder, and Salia jumped in, followed by Lady Alouette and the dragons. Salia heard the same noises she heard last time. Dripping water, and she could've sworn she heard screaming. She thought it must've been bad memories. Salia kept her thoughts open to Star, struggling to keep her eyes closed. If she opened her eyes, she would sever her connection. As she followed Star's thoughts, she thought about all of the unanswered questions.

Why she couldn't stay with the MoonWings.

Who really is Kalista and Alvann?

What is The Starborne planning to do?

Who is Lady Alouette's other identity?

There were so many more. But there was one that they needed to focus on.

Where is Star?

Salia was about to say something when a voice around her echoed off of the small, dark room.

"Looking for someone?"

Salia immediately recognized the voice as Kalista.

"What do you want?" Salia asked.

"I want to know what you're doing back here. Oh, let me guess. Your precious Star went missing."

"What have you done with her?" Snowdrift growled.

"Good to see you, too, Snowdrift." Kalista said.

"Where are you?" Salia asked.

"And you think I would tell you? Shouldn't you be looking for Star before she's dead? Unless she already is."

"Where is she?" Salia demanded.

"Did you miss me?"

"I would never miss you." Salia said.

"Of course you wouldn't. When will you start making the right choices? When will you join us?"

"Never," Salia said.

"Your best friend Calalynn is doing great here."

"She is *not* my best friend. She probably killed Star!" Salia yelled.

Snowdrift backed up.

"What makes you think it was her?"

"She told us!" Salia yelled.

Kalista laughed. "Well, then. Have fun finding your precious Star. She's probably dead, anyway. And one wrong move, you'll be dead, too."

Kalista's voice faded away.

Snowdrift looked like she wanted to cry. "Let's go. She might not be alive -- she choked on those words -- but we still have to find her."

Salia felt Star getting closer. "She's this way!"

They walked through the forked hallway, eager to run. But she was too afraid of making it collapse again.

"Which way?" Lady Alouette asked.

Salia took a long, deep breath. "Right."

"I'll go in first." Lady Alouette said.

The room was darker than every room in the cavern, except a flicker of blue light. Lady Alouette gasped. Everyone ran into the room at once.

"What?" Salia asked when all she saw was darkness. Lady Alouette had her hands over her mouth. Then she saw what she was looking at.

A limp, unconscious, bloody Star, laying on the ground with a note laying right beside her.

It was your chance to get her.

Now it's our chance to get you.

EPILOGUE

"WE GOT HER!" ALVANN SAID, AS KALISTA carried Calalynn into Starlight Caverns. Calalynn was bleeding all over.

"Salia Lightsinged all of us," Kalista said. "Luckily, we were prepared and jumped into the water."

"Still, that wasn't a very good idea," Alvann pulled up the sleeve on his black cloak, showing his scratches and burns.

"Oh, please. It was a much better idea than what they did!" Kalista pointed to Calalynn's unconscious body. "They nearly died."

Alvann nodded. "I didn't know Salia could Lightsinge."

"Neither did I. But Salia's still at Jewel Academy, with the MoonWings, and Star. I thought I told you to kill her!" Kalista said.

"She might be dead already!" Alvann said.

"True. But she's not who we're going after."

"I know what you're going to say. We have to go after Salia and the MoonWings."

"Yes, but not just them. Soon, the entire elvin world is going to regret that they never joined our order."

"What are you going to do?"

"Something. But I'm not going to do it alone."

"Of course I'll help you. But what are you going to do?"

"Alvann, don't you get it? They're under our control! And soon, every single one of them will be."

ACKNOWLEDGEMENTS

Yay -- you're still here! And you're still reading! I know this wasn't as good as KOTLC or Wings Of Fire, but I really hoped you all liked it! A lot of credit to Shannon Messenger and Tui T. Sutherland :) Remember to look out for the next books! Book 2: MoonWing - Starborne! So I have to say thank you to a lot of people!

Thank you to Shannon Messenger, for writing KOTLC and inspiring me to do this. I love your books so much!

Thank you to Tui T. Sutherland, for writing Wings Of Fire and inspiring me to do this. I love your books so much!

Thank you to Eleni, the best co - editor ever and author of The Starborne! And for always being there for me! Thank you for being the best friend ever!

Thank you to Corinne Luck, for your guidance in this process!

Thank you to my publishers, for making this book happen!

Thank you to Ashton, for being there for me! Thank you for being the best friend ever!

Thank you to Drew, for being a great friend!

Thank you to Mom, for always being there for me! I love you!

Thank you to Dad, for always being there for me! I love you!

Thank you to Caitlin, for being the obnoxious, sarcastic, amazing older sister you are! I love you!

Thank you to Ginger, for being the best puppy in the world! I love you!

Thank you to my entire family, for always being there for me! I love you!

Thank you to my readers, for reading this and making me so happy! Thank you!

There are so many more people to thank, and thank you to everyone! :)

Made in the USA
Middletown, DE
04 April 2021